THE KING

LIGHTNING McQUEEN

SHERIFF

DOC HUDSON

CHICK

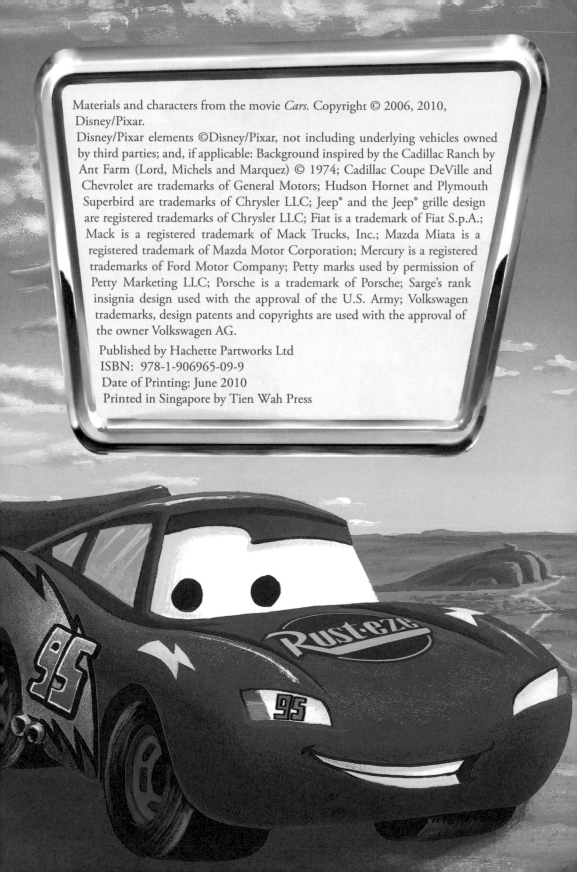

Published by Hachette Partworks Ltd
ISBN: 978-1-906965-09-9
Date of Printing: June 2010
Printed in Singapore by Tien Wah Press

Disney·PIXAR
Hachette

Welcome to the biggest race of the year! To the hotshot rookie racer Lightning McQueen, it was everything he had ever worked for. Once Lightning won the Piston Cup, he would get all the fame and fortune he had always dreamed of. To Lightning, this race was *all* about winning.

It would not be an easy victory for Lightning. The King, the current champion, was doing his best to win. And the rough racer Chick was doing his worst! Chick hated coming in second place, and he wouldn't stop at dirty tricks to beat Lightning.

But Lightning had a daring plan. As everyone else pulled into pit row for a change of tyres, Lightning pushed on! It was a risky move – too risky. BLAM! BLAM! As he was heading for victory, his two rear tyres blew.

The King and Chick caught right up with Lightning!

What a race!

"That was quite a risky move, not taking tyres," a reporter said to Lightning. "Are you sorry that you don't have a crew chief?"

"No," said Lightning, " 'cause I'm a one-man show!"

The King offered the rookie some advice. "You ain't gonna win unless you got good folks behind you," The King said. "Racing ain't a one man deal."

Then the announcers reported the results. It was a three-way tie! Now the race had to be settled at a rematch in California.

Lightning was very disappointed. If his tyres hadn't blown, he would probably have won. Lightning boarded Mack's trailer and they took off. Wanting to be the first one to arrive in California so he could practice, Lightning said, "We're driving straight through all night!"

"I don't think I can make it!" said Mack. He was so tired that he could barely keep his eyes open.

"Oh, sure you can," said Lightning. But soon they both fell asleep and neither of them noticed when Lightning fell off the trailer!

"Ahhhh!" Lightning yelled when he woke up driving the wrong way into traffic. Totally confused, the panicked car sped through the little town of Radiator Springs. Unfortunately, Lightning was going way, way too fast.

He lost control of his wheels and got tangled
in a fence. With the town's sheriff hot on his tail,
Lightning caught hold of a statue and tore up the
road. Oh boy! Lightning was in a lot of trouble now.

"Morning, sleepin' beauty!" yelled a happy tow truck, when Lightning awoke the next morning.

"What's going on here?" Lightning gasped, as he finally realised that he was trapped in the town's impound lot.

Mater, the tow truck, smiled back at him from outside the fence. "You're funny, I like you already," Mater said. "You're in Radiator Springs, the cutest little town in Carburetor County!"

Lightning looked through the fence. It didn't look so cute to him. All he saw were a few empty, broken-down buildings.

Lightning was towed to the courthouse, where he faced an angry crowd. Lightning was certain they would let him go, once they realised he was a famous race car. How wrong Lightning was!

Doc Hudson, the town doctor and judge, wanted Lightning out of town. But Sally, the town attorney, convinced Doc that Lightning should stay and fix the road.

"You're going to fix the road under my supervision!" ruled Doc.

"You gotta be kidding me!" Lightning said.

Lightning protested, but there was no way out.
"This here is Bessie – finest road-pavin'
machine ever built," said Doc proudly. He
pointed to an enormous piece of machinery.
"Hook him up, Mater!"

There was plenty of work for Lightning to do. He would have to hurry, if he was going to make it to California in time for the big race. And the race was the most important thing in Lightning's life right now.

At first, Lightning didn't care whether he did a good job or not. He just had to finish so he could leave town. In one hour, he was done.

"It looks awful!" said Sally. "Now it matches the rest of the town," Lightning replied, trying to be funny.

"The deal was you fix the road, not make it worse," grumbled Doc, when he saw the results of Lightning's efforts.
"Start over again!"

"I'm not a bulldozer, I'm a race car," said Lightning.

Doc stared right at Lightning and offered him a challenge: "Then why don't we have a little race – me and you."

"If you win,
you go. If I win,
you do the road
my way," said
Doc. Everyone
was surprised.
How was Doc
ever going to win?
They all went to
a place just outside
Radiator Springs called
Willy's Butte. As soon as the
race began, Lightning left
Doc in a cloud of dust.
Everyone looked at Doc,
who slowly pulled away
from the starting line.
"Come on, Mater," he
said, rolling along.
"Might need a
little help."

And sure enough, help *was* needed. Lightning was heading for a turn when he skidded and lost control. Lightning dropped off a low cliff and landed right in a cactus patch. Ouch!

"I'm starting to think he knowed you was gonna crash," giggled Mater as he pulled Lightning back up.

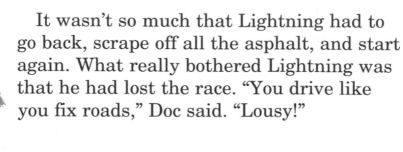

It wasn't so much that Lightning had to go back, scrape off all the asphalt, and start again. What really bothered Lightning was that he had lost the race. "You drive like you fix roads," Doc said. "Lousy!"

Lightning was a proud race car, and he didn't want to be called lousy by anyone.

"I'll show him. I *will* show him," he thought to himself. And then Lightning went to work on the road – much more determined than before.

The next morning, the town awoke to a newly paved section of road. It was beautiful!

"Wow," said Sally.

Even Doc looked impressed, but he still didn't trust Lightning. "He ain't finished yet," Doc said. "Now, where the heck is he?"

Lightning was out at Willy's Butte! He wanted to learn to make the turn he had missed.

Doc couldn't help smiling as Lightning stumbled on the turn again and again. After a while, Doc offered Lightning some advice: turn right to go left. When Doc wasn't looking, Lightning tried it – and he missed the turn again!

Meanwhile, inspired by the new road, all the cars in the town began fixing their shops, making them prettier than ever.

Sally saw
the effect
Lightning's hard
work was having
on the town and
wanted to thank him.
She invited him to stay at her
motel, so he wouldn't have to
sleep at the dirty impound
lot any more.

"Hey, I know somethin' we can do," Mater said that night. Lightning had no idea what the silly tow truck was up to but it would probably be fun.

Soon they were sneaking into a field of sleeping tractors just outside of Radiator Springs. Yup! They were going tractor tipping!

"Just don't let Frank catch you!" warned Mater.

"Who's Frank?" asked Lightning, but Mater had already honked his horn. A sleeping tractor tipped over with a snort. Lightning, who didn't have a horn, revved his engine. Dozens of tractors tipped! Mater and Lightning laughed and laughed – until a huge harvester appeared and charged them!

"That's Frank!" screamed Mater.

The next morning, Lightning peeked into Doc's
back garage. To Lightning's surprise, he found
three Piston Cups hidden in all of the clutter. Doc
used to be a famous race car!

At that
moment, Doc
arrived. Furious
that Lightning
had discovered his
secret, Doc shooed the rookie
away, slamming the door in
Lightning's face.

Lightning was very confused. Why would a famous race car stop racing and settle down in a sleepy town?

Later that day, Lightning found Doc racing at Willy's Butte. Doc was amazing. But when he saw Lightning, Doc turned around and headed home.

"How could a car like you quit at the top of your game?" Lightning asked, after following Doc back to the garage.

"I didn't quit. They quit on ME!" Doc said bitterly. He had been damaged in a big wreck; and when he returned, a talented rookie – just like Lightning – had taken Doc's place. After that, Doc didn't trust race cars.

"Just finish that road and get outta here," Doc said.

Lightning worked all night to finish the road. Soon the little town looked shiny and new, with neon signs lighting the main street. The cars were very proud.

But, just as all the cars began cruising up and down main street, they were interrupted. A helicopter and a flood of journalists arrived. They had been searching high and low for Lightning – and now they had found him!

Mack was also there. "I'm so sorry I lost you, boss!" he said. Lightning didn't know how to say goodbye to his new friends. Sadly, he slipped into his trailer and headed off to the big race. The reporters left. And the townsfolk turned off the neon signs. Just as quickly as he had arrived, Lightning was gone again.

Finally it was race day! The King, Chick, and Lightning were waiting at the starting line, ready for the final race for this year's Piston Cup series. But Lightning had a hard time keeping his mind on the track. He missed his friends in Radiator Springs.

Lightning was close to giving up, when suddenly
a voice called out on his radio: "I didn't come all this
way to see you quit!" It was Doc! "I knew you needed
a crew chief, but I didn't know it was this bad."

What!? Doc had pulled a crew
together from Radiator Springs
– and now they were going to
help Lightning win the race.

Lightning drove his best ever; but just as he passed Chick, the bully bumped into Lightning's back and sent him spinning towards the infield. Lightning recovered using the advice Doc had given him back at the dirt track: turn right to go left. Lightning shot back onto the track – and into the lead!

Chick was furious. "I'm not coming in last," he yelled, and rammed straight into The King! The old champion crashed.

Lightning was shocked. It reminded him of Doc. This was no way for The King to end his glorious career.

Inches before the finish line, Lightning slammed on his brakes, turned around, and went back to help The King finish his final race.

"Yeah! Whoo-hoo I won!" hollered Chick, but no one noticed him. Everyone was busy cheering Lightning and The King. Lightning had given up winning the race, proving he was a true champion. Doc couldn't have been prouder.

Lightning set up his new racing headquarters at Radiator Springs. Doc was his new crew chief and occasional racing partner. It seemed the hotshot rookie still had a lot to learn from the old timer. Lightning felt so good to be among friends again.

THE END